If You Expect The Unexpected, Then It Won't Be Unexpected Anymore: A Perfectly (Un)Expected Collection of Short Stories.

By Matty Millard

ISBN: 978-0-9926971-7-4
Published by Off The Shelf Publishing Ltd

THE STORIES

Matty Millard

AN ANGEL IN THE NIGHT

"No, please don't," I whined. My friend Sian had decided that it had been far too long since I'd had a girlfriend, and she was going to do something about it. "It's embarrassing when you try and set me up, you always make me look really stupid."

"That's not true!" she insisted. "You do that well enough by yourself."

I laughed and flicked some of my beer at her, and she feigned offence. She was right, I could never think of anything to say when I spoke to girls I liked, but having Sian there watching me **added** pressure – it didn't take it away. I managed to change the course of conversation to how bad her taste in girls was anyway, I'm sure she only ever introduced me to the girls she didn't fancy herself.

It was always going to be one of those nights. It was a Friday, the day after payday, and town was packed. We began in our usual haunt, The Red Lion, an old-man pub close to the station. We liked it in there, it had a good selection of ales, was relatively unpretentious and it was quiet enough to have a decent chat before moving on to somewhere more lively.

Around midnight Steve suggested we went to the Subway Club, a dark dingy nightclub, which played alternative and heavy metal music until 6 am. We were all keen to go, but made the usual pact that we would leave at around 2 so that we weren't too hung-over. Everyone knew that was a hollow agreement. We'd be there as long as we could stand up, if not longer.

As we approached the entrance I waved at a familiar face.

"Hey Marshall," grinned the skinhead on the door. "Must be payday, good to see you!"

"Are we that predictable?" I asked, shaking his outstretched hand.

"Like clockwork mate. Busy tonight, have a good one."

I walked up the steps, passing my five pounds to the girl at the window before walking into the club. The heavy bass of a Rammstein track was pounding out, and it gave me that sense of elation I get every time I enter a bar like that. It feels instantly like home. An atmosphere of complete comfort, somewhere you won't be judged.

The others followed, and after a couple of shots of Jager we hit the dance floor. That's when I spotted her. She was sitting at the bar, alone except for the glass of vodka and ice in front of her. She looked so serene and peaceful, a classical beauty with high cheekbones and not a blemish on her skin. Her black lipstick and short black hair gave her an air of intrigue and mystery.

I didn't even realise I had been staring until Sian kicked me in the shin.

"Ow!" I cried, spilling half of my beer on the floor. "What was that for?"

"Why don't you go and speak to her?" she asked. "She's pretty."

"I will, later," I replied, not really meaning it. I don't like to make a fool of myself and she was way out of my league. I glanced up at her again, and she smiled. I wasn't sure it was at me, but I half-smiled and half-blushed back just in case. I hoped she hadn't seen me spill my drink everywhere.

For the next hour or so I carried on dancing with my

friends, but I couldn't quite shake her out of my mind. I glanced at her once or twice, and she was still sat there, alone. I'd noticed a few guys approach her over the night, but she'd waved them away with barely a word.

Eventually it was my round again so I went to the bar.

"Three beers and a red wine please."

I delivered the wine and two beers to my friends and went back to collect the one I couldn't carry.

I glanced along the bar again, and the girl waved at me. I waved back, and smiled. I knew I should go over, but I still paused long enough for her to pat the chair next to her. Ok, I looked a bit lame but at least I now knew she definitely wanted to talk to me.

Ok, think of something interesting to say. What does she do? No that's boring. Music. Ask her what bands she likes.

I sat down and placed my beer carefully on the bar.

"Hey," I said. "I'm Marshall."

"Letitia," she replied, offering a delicate hand with a single brass ornamented ring on the little finger.

I took it. "Nice to meet you," I said. *Original.*

She laughed. "I notice that you've been looking at me a lot tonight."

My heart dropped. *She thinks I'm a freak and a pervert.* "I.. err… I was trying to summon up the courage to come and say hi. You're really pretty," I blurted.

"Thanks," she smiled. "I'm glad you made it over here…Eventually."

I relaxed instantly, she had just been teasing.

"So, where are you from?" I asked.

"Where do I start?" she laughed, an honest and carefree sound. "I was born in Romania where I lived until I was a teenager when my mother got a job in France. I pretty much followed her around Europe, living in Germany, the Czech Republic and Slovenia before we came to the UK."

"Wow, so you like to travel?"

It turned out she did, and she travelled to music festivals and concerts all around the world. She had toured with a band for a summer as a roadie. Since she had stopped travelling she had done a degree to become a vet, before retraining to become a nurse. Now she had aspirations of volunteering in an African wildlife sanctuary.

We sat chatting for what could have been hours. She was fascinating and we had so much in common. On top of being the most interesting person I think I'd ever met, she drank vodka straight and spoke with a passion, a confidence and a tenacity that left me spellbound.

"I see your friends have left," she said.

"Oh, have they?" I hadn't noticed. I glanced at my phone, I had one message. *Gone home. Didn't want to disturb, you seem to be getting on well. Good work! Sian x.* "They've sent me a text, you're right."

"So, I guess you're coming home with me then?"

The lump in my throat came back again. I tried to form some words but they came out as a silent "errr…"

"What? Don't you want to?" she feigned offence, but I could tell she was simply amused by my shyness. I didn't usually do this on first meetings, but I would have been really stupid not to roll with it.

"Yeah, of course. Thanks. That would be great."

She laughed, and stood up for the first time, to reveal a long black dress which hugged her hourglass figure. I was gobsmacked, she really was the girl of my dreams.

"Come on then," she said, linking her arm with mine.

I walked with her to find a taxi in a bit of a haze. I didn't notice the broken bottles in the gutter, the drunken louts staggering around with their grease-filled boxes of chips, or the opportunist thieves standing on the street corner. I was in a different world, seeing the city without its many imperfections for a change. It wasn't long until we jumped into a car, for the short journey to her place.

***

Letitia unlocked a huge wooden front door with a large leaden key. I followed her into her home, along the corridor into the kitchen.

She opened a cupboard, and pulled out a decanter of wine. "Would you like a glass?"

I nodded, so she filled it to the top. We'd had plenty to drink already, but I'd have felt rude to turn down the offer. She selected a different wine, and poured her own glass.

"I prefer the cheap stuff, the good wine is for guests."

She beckoned me to follow her into the spacious living room, where I sat on the end of a dark leather couch.

"Come here, I don't bite!" she laughed, and I budged up the sofa towards her. "Unless you want me to, of course." I squirmed, not knowing how to answer so swigged my wine to offset my nervousness.

Letitia leant into my shoulder and we quickly settled back into comfortable chatter and sipped on our wine. She told me about her early life back in Romania as a child.

"We never had a TV," she said. "So when we were kids we pretended to be werewolves, or phantoms or vampires. It was fun, but we had to be careful not to play in front of certain people. Many still believe in these creatures, especially in the rural areas. It's far more than just folklore out there."

"I guess it's like our own King Arthur," I replied, knowing that it wasn't. "We all know the stories are fictitious, but the person they all stemmed from must have existed or been inspired by someone real. I wonder how these tales began?"

Another hour or so must have passed before Letitia looked at her watch. I found it refreshing – she hadn't looked at her phone once all night, and it was rare to find someone who wore a watch nowadays. Maybe she just didn't have an interest in technology. She had a television and a cd player, but none of the endless amounts of gadgets that you usually see in a twenty-something's house nowadays. Letitia's house was traditional, with wood-panelled walls and grand leaded windows. She had huge brass candlesticks on the fireplace. It definitely complemented her love of gothic fashion and music.

"Oh no!" she cried. "Is that really the time?"

I knew it was late, my eyes had been getting heavier and heavier for a while. It was 06:50, and the very first few rays of sunlight had begun to show. She stood up, and hurried over to the windows, drawing the curtains carefully.

"I think it's about time we went to bed, don't you?" she asked, sitting back down next to me.

Before I'd even had time to nod, she grabbed my t-shirt and pulled me to her, kissing me passionately. I kissed her back, cursing myself for being so tired. I was seriously struggling to keep my eyes open. She pushed me down onto the settee, pulled my t-shirt up and over my head, and clambered onto me. I lay on my back, heart pounding as she kissed my face, my neck and my chest. She looked into my half-closed eyes, and smiled. I smiled back as her lips caressed my neck once more.

They lingered there for a moment, and that's all I remember.

***

I woke up the following day, on the settee in a strange house, all alone.

My head was banging, my limbs ached, and there was a terrible dull pain in my neck from the arm-rest my head had been on. I looked at my phone, it was the middle of the afternoon. I'd clearly passed out properly last night. I could feel the queasiness of my hangover kicking in, I really needed to get home to my own bed. I stood up, and instantly felt dizzy and sick.

But I couldn't leave without saying goodbye to Letitia.

I searched the house from top to bottom, but there was no sign of her. She must have been so annoyed with me for falling asleep that she had gone out without wanting to speak to me.

Spying a letter on the floor by the front door, I found her address and ordered a taxi to come and pick me up. I sat wallowing in my misery until it arrived. I couldn't believe how spectacularly I had messed this up.

I got a text telling me that my taxi was here, so I shut the front door behind me and got in the car. I grimaced as I pulled the seatbelt over my shoulder, my neck was really tender.

"Are you ok?" asked the driver, turning my attention to a stain on my t-shirt. It was blood, only a tiny bit but it was obvious against my white shirt. Somehow I'd not noticed it before, but I wasn't that concerned, I'm clumsy and seem to pick up mystery drinking injuries all the time.

"Yeah I'm fine, thanks. Just a bit of a scratch, I need to go home and clean up." I shivered and zipped up my coat, hiding the stain away.

It wasn't long before I got home, and I tried to creep into the house. I didn't really feel like talking to any of my friends. There was no chance of that happening though, our front door was really squeaky.

"Here he is!" cried Steve as I walked in. "The dirty stop out!"

"Yeah yeah, whatever," I replied.

"You don't look very happy," said Sian. "What happened?"

"I don't wanna talk about it," I said, and I went upstairs and closed myself into the safe solitude of my room. Throwing myself down on the bed I lay there, inwardly cursing my idiocy. Letitia was the most incredible girl I'd ever met, and I'd completely blown it. *How difficult is it to stay awake? Come on!*

Dozing in and out of sleep for a few hours made me feel almost human again, so I got up and had a shower to complete the transformation.

I got out and dried myself, and brushed my teeth in front of the mirror. *That's strange,* I thought, noticing a blotch on the side of my neck. Looking at it closer, it was actually two round holes, close together, surrounded by bruising. I had no idea where they had come from, but at least it explained the throbbing pain I'd had, and the blood on my t-shirt.

So it was whilst I lay on my bed flicking through the channels that the thoughts entered my head. *True Blood* was showing on one side. I groaned, and changed channel to be greeted by *An Interview With A Vampire.* It was while I half-watched *Count Duckula,* a cartoon from my childhood that the seed was planted. I shrugged it off to start with, but the more I thought about it, the more it made sense. *Could Letitia be a vampire?* It wasn't just the cuts on my neck, there were plenty of other signs. She had reacted with some shock when she had seen how close to morning and daylight it was, and she must have been hidden away from the light when I woke up. She had achieved an awful lot in her life having been a vet, a nurse and a roadie, but only looked to be in her twenties. Her house was full of old, antiquated things, the taste that someone would have if they were hundreds of years old. She was from Romania – where all the vampires came from. And the last thing I remember was falling asleep, with her kissing my neck. I touched my neck again. It stung. And my theory made so much sense.

I didn't really know how to react. I couldn't tell my friends, they'd think I'd gone mad and would blame it all on the drink. Besides, they'd never let me forget an accusation like that.

I switched on my computer and Googled *"Are there vampires in Birmingham?"* I hoped it would tell me that I was being stupid and that vampires don't exist, but according to the internet they do and there had been lots of people bitten recently. *Thanks, freedom of information.*

Turning off the monitor in a huff, I decided to go to bed. I needed to sleep on it before I jumped to any hasty conclusions.

***

Sleeping on it didn't really go to plan. I lay awake all night, thoughts flying through my head. *Did Letitia really bite me? If she is is an actual vampire, might I become a vampire? Do vampires even exist, she's probably just a weird gothic fan-girl? I'm going to be a vampire. You're being an idiot, they're fictional. Do I need to drink blood now? Will I live for ever? I'm never going to be able to eat garlic bread again!*

The sleep never came. I worked myself into more and more of a panic, thinking of all of the questions that I had to ask Letitia tomorrow. Morning came and I rose, eyes red from lack of sleep. I didn't have a wash, I didn't stop to have breakfast, I didn't greet any of my friends. I didn't know or care whether I was delusional, I just walked downstairs to my car, and drove to Letitia's house.

Knocking on the door, I waited with apprehension. There was no reply. Obviously, if she was a vampire she couldn't open the door in daylight. But I was frantic, I had to get in. I tried the handle, and wiggled it from side to side. I put my shoulder to the door and pushed gently, gauging its strength.

"Excuse me. What do you think you are you doing?"

I span around, startled. There was a plump, middle-aged lady staring at me with her hands on her hips. She didn't look best pleased.

"Erm… I'm trying to get in. It's locked."

"I can see that. Who are you?"

"I'm Marshall. A friend of Letitia's. She's not been returning my calls – I was worried. And you?"

"I'm her maid. It's a big house and she doesn't get enough time to keep it herself."

I bet she doesn't, I thought.

"She'll be asleep now, you'll need to come back later."

Of course she will, vampires sleep in the daytime. I nodded glumly, my suspicions were being confirmed. "When?" I found myself asking.

***

I sat at home in my room, thinking about the situation all day long. I played the situation over and over in my head. None of the situations I imagined had good endings. Eventually the time came, 9pm. I drove, grimly, across town and knocked on Letitia's door. She opened it and gasped at the sight of me, hammer raised in my right hand above my head. I'd come prepared, grasping a wooden stake in the other, with garlic and a crucifix hung around my neck. I forced my way in and she scampered back, a look of horror on her face.

"What are you doing?" she screamed. "Get away from me!"

"You know what you've done," I stated, coldly. "I want some answers, now – before I make certain that you can't do it to anyone else."

She backed away along the corridor, and tripped over the vacuum cleaner. She lay on her back, shaking uncontrollably.

"I'm sorry!" she cried, bursting into tears. "I can explain."

"You don't need to explain. You're a vampire and it's in your nature to drink my blood. But that doesn't mean I'll let you get away with it."

I knelt over her, the point of my stake close to her chest.

"Please don't!" she whispered. "I'm not a vampire!"

"Really?" I sneered. "Well explain this then." I pulled down my collar to show the two red marks that had appeared the night I met Letitia.

"Ok," she replied, her voice shaking. "But you're not going to like it."

That wasn't the response I had expected, and it took me by surprise. There was a sincerity in her voice that made me want to trust her. I banished from my mind all thoughts of what would happen to me if I was wrong, and I stood. She scrabbled backwards, pushing herself to her feet.

Letitia walked towards the kitchen, and motioned for me to follow. She dragged a cupboard away from the wall to reveal a trapdoor down to a cellar. If she was a vampire, I knew I was being really stupid by following her down there, but I had given her a chance so I had to go with it now. Besides, she seemed far more scared of me than a vampire should be.

When we reached the bottom of the cellar steps we walked straight to a fridge at the side of the room. Letitia opened the door revealing vials of blood. "I got this off the black market, but I'm still short. Type AB's hard to come by."

I stared at her, a silent anger raging behind my confusion.

"You're type AB," she continued. "I tested you last night and I drugged you so that you wouldn't remember. I put the two spots in your neck so you'd think I was just a wanna-be vamp goth kid. There's loads of weirdoes out there nowadays that'll give you a bite. I didn't take any yet, I promise, but I was going to call you later and see if you could help."

She walked over to a full-length curtain which she drew back slowly. Inside was a bed, surrounded by medical equipment. A drip was attached to an underweight and elderly lady, who was unconscious and clearly very weak.

"This is my Mother. She's already had three liver transplants. The hospitals won't treat her anymore because she won't give up the liquor. She's only forty five. I need two more pints before I can try and give her a transfusion."

My rage disappeared as I looked into the desperate, loving eyes of the vampire girl I had met two days ago.

I didn't know what to say, so I just sat down and rolled my sleeve up.

Matty Millard

Weapons of Mass Destruction

Hey! I'm Rotten Johnny, and you join me, panting for breath as I rest against the school gate.

Today was the biggest day of the Old Carrions Grammar School calendar, Finals Day for the all-important conker season.

I'm pretty good at conkers if I do say so myself. In fact, I'm the best.

I joined Old Carrions three years ago, and in all that time I have never been beaten. This year I was going to buy a new trophy cabinet from my winnings, but I don't think it will be necessary any more.

I know, I'm not making a lot of sense. So let me start from the beginning.

The bell rang for lunchtime, and I ran outside, excited for my Grand Final. A crowd of mainly twelve and thirteen year olds had already formed around the school clock tower where the final is always played. I'm sixteen, and I know I'm a little old to still be playing conkers but it's different at Old Carrions to other schools. Elsewhere it's just kids swinging a horse-chestnut on a shoelace to break another conker, but it isn't just a game at Old Carrions Grammar School. Conkers is a lifestyle.

At the edge of the crowd I was swamped by kids wishing me luck and trading high fives. So many different people love conkers at Old Carrions, it turns a school into a real community. Poor kids play because it's the only form of entertainment they can afford. Groups of jocks are all fist pumps and bravado, they get really het up in the excitement. Others just like the tradition.

There's also the groupies, who drive me mad. Most don't care about conkers, they just want to know the popular kids in school. As reigning champion I put up with loads of these. I can handle the attentions of the ladies, of course, but there are only so many times I can answer that bloody question the newbies ask, "should I aim for the top, or the side of the conker?"

It doesn't matter, just welly it!

Porky Pete grabbed both my arms as I pushed my way through the crowd.

"Please Johnny, you've got to win!" he whispered, stress lines etched across his face.

Porky Pete's one of the worst kind of groupies, the "Stattos". His briefcase is stuffed full of analyses of conker matches, player's form, history between rivals, performance records on windy days. He studies everything, he's obsessed.

"I will, don't worry," I told him. I knew the reason for his worries. Porky Pete had staked all of his savings on the Grand Final, and feared asking his parents for more dinner money. There would be loads more kids behind the clock tower too, trying to place a last minute bet. I was 25-1 to win within three swings, generous odds and a popular bet. This, of course, wouldn't happen as I both "regulate" and fund the bookies thanks to the hundreds of pounds I make from selling the conkers off my parents' tree.

Conkers is easy money. Without conkers I couldn't afford the Doc Marten boots I wear to school every day, or the strong hair wax which glues my fringe in position. My Mom would never buy me these things so I have to make my own money. I'm not daft though, I don't sell the best conkers. The biggest and the hardest ones I keep for myself.

It's not all riches though, I've had a few uncomfortable situations with losing customers too. My friend Dangerous Dave, a stocky sixth former, once saved me from drowning in the toilets after Harry "Crusher" Harris lost one of the biggest wagers I have ever seen. Ever since, he's been the head of my notorious "Enforcer" bodyguards.

A scuffle breaks out further forward in the crowd, so I leave Porky Pete and fight my way into the middle of two boys who are going tooth and nail at each other. I don't know them, but they recognise me and stand back.

"Rotten Johnny", says a distraught first year holding a conker-less shoelace. "You're not allowed to play 'stamps' at Old Carrions are you?"

"Absolutely not!" I replied. 'Stamps' is a controversial rule only allowed by barbarians of the game, where you are allowed to stamp on an opponent's conker if they drop it on the floor. I raised my hand and Dangerous Dave dragged the offender out of the crowd to teach him a well-deserved lesson.

I had almost reached the clock-tower when I felt another hand on my shoulder. Constant attention is the price you pay for being a Champion. Sighing, I turned to face an agitated first year.

"What now?"

"Rotten Johnny, can you moderate a deal for me? He wants me to pay ten pounds for this conker. It's not even drilled!"

I glanced at the shiny new watch on my wrist. "Come to me after the match," I replied. "We start in three minutes."

As you can see, I own the conker world. I started and

hence run the thriving black market. I vet the quality of conkers to ensure no-one gets ripped off. I determine the market value per gram of conker. Earlier in the season, strange betting patterns forced my Enforcers and I to close down a match fixing scandal after clear favourite Steve "the Smasher" Wallace missed his opponent's conker and hit a wall under absolutely no pressure at all. An injury gained in "mysterious" circumstances meant that he still hadn't managed to use the brand new football boots he had brought to school the following day.

Through my Enforcers, I ensure that everyone else plays fair. But nobody monitors Rotten Johnny.

I have been selling counterfeit conkers for almost two years now. 95% of the conker swinging community of Old Carrions Grammar School have bought some form of contraband item smuggled in a conker shell from me, whether chewing gum (the illogically prohibited scourge of Grammar schools), or a photo of a girl from a naughty magazine. The most recent addition to my portfolio is the sale of conkers stuffed with cocaine, and quite frankly I'm laughing all the way to the bank.

I finally got through the crowds and reached the clock tower, where I winked at my best customer. Charlie the Conqueror hates me bitterly, and I have to say the feeling is mutual. Charlie is both jealous and a terrible loser, as he demonstrates annually when I beat him in the Old Carrions Grammar School Grand Final.

Earlier in the term, I sold him a gram of cocaine so that he could temporarily forget his woes. Every lunchtime nowadays, I see him doing a line behind the bike sheds. Each time he buys from me, he tells me how much he hates giving me money. I just smile, because he keeps coming back.

Today is a showcase for sport, not business, so I extend my hand to Charlie. In return I get a vitriolic stare. A hush descends across the crowd. They want to hear what is said, everyone knows our history.

The 2012 Grand Final had finished with some rather ugly scenes when Charlie the Conqueror had publicly questioned my ethics. Everybody knows there is a widespread problem in the game with competitors baking conkers, soaking them in vinegar or varnishing them to get a head-start, but to suggest that the conker of the most respected man in the game is a fake was just way out of line.

I had feared more trouble this time, as Charlie had far more at stake than last year. I hadn't stopped selling coke to Charlie when he had run out of money. I hadn't stopped selling to him when he had pawned all of his heavy metal CD's, but I did stop selling to him when Charlie had said that all he owned were the clothes on his back, and the conker in his pocket.

I couldn't take his clothes, nobody wants to see that. And taking a stricken man's conker is just bad form. I have absolutely no problem with gallantly smashing it into tiny little pieces though, and that was exactly what I planned to do today.

Charlie the Conqueror was equally desperate to win, as if he did he would make £500 from the bookies. That would buy him a lot of cocaine.

The bell rang to signify it was one o' clock, and more importantly, it was time to start the Grand Final. The tension was palpable.

Charlie won the coin toss and elected to go first. He hit with each of his first three swings, and celebrated to the applause of the crowd. I repeated the pattern, and bowed as the roars intensified. Charlie continued the trend for his next two, but on the second hit a small flake of shell fell from his conker. His face was awash with annoyance.

"Rotten Johnny should be disqualified," announced Charlie. "He sells trick conkers."

A general murmuring rumbled around the playground. Everyone knew it was true, but the lack of outrage indicated that people were okay with it. The world of conkers was about far more than just winning a tournament after all.

I grinned, knowing that it would force a rise out of Charlie. "Charlie, I knew you were desperate but this is really clutching at straws. I know you're losing, but trying to get **me** disqualified for selling **you** conkers full of coke will never work!"

Charlie would have been better off if he had tempered his irritation. He wouldn't have won the match, but he would have looked like a far more competent conker player had his anger not taken his focus from accuracy to power.

I laughed heartily as Charlie's wayward conker missed mine, wrapped around his arm and struck his own knuckles. I swung my "Weapon of Mass Destruction", as it had been dubbed, three times with power and accuracy. As he cursed openly, Charlie's hopes lay on the ground in a smashed mess of conker and shell.

"You win again," Charlie stated forlornly, but I could see that he wasn't finished. "But I think you'll find, that after three years of undefeated conker playing, we must insist on breaking your conker to check what's inside."

I knew there was no argument I could have with this statement. It was clearly stipulated in the rules that the conker used must be from the present year's harvest, so I would have no further use for this one. A quick glance towards Dangerous Dave confirmed this.

It was all over. I couldn't stay whilst they uncovered the truth, the consequences would be catastrophic. I ran out of Old Carrions as fast as I possibly could, pushing past and trying to ignore the stunned faces of the crowd. After three glorious years, I had finally been found out.

Behind me, Charlie placed the conker on the floor and raised a stone in the air. I can only imagine the glee he must have felt as he prepared to expose my scandal to the whole school.

Stopping to catch my breath, I leaned on the school gate and looked back from where I had run. As the metal casing inside my conker split, the chemicals inside it mixed freely. I saw the explosion rip the slate roof off the clock tower. Flames and smoke engulfed the old leaded windows of Old Carrions.

I've been standing here for about five minutes now, and I've come to a decision. There is still a lot to be said for conkers, and I'm definitely getting better at it.

I just need to get through that awkward conversation with my Dad first, about how I need to go to a new school because my current one has exploded and everyone has died, again.

"But this time, Dad, could you *please* send me to that private school in the hills where all the rich kids go?"

Matty Millard

An Eclair Story

"Stupid bloody machine yow am," cursed Darren as he slammed the phone down.

It wasn't the phone's fault that Darren had spent all of his money on a really dirty kebab that he would definitely regret in the morning. Phone boxes weren't in the habit of giving out free phone calls.

Darren stumbled out of the phone box back into the writhing mess of drunken partygoers that was Birmingham's Broad Street, kicking the door shut behind him. He wasn't happy, to put it mildly. Just twenty minutes ago he'd left the club he was in after a girl he'd been chatting up had tipped a pint of cider over him. That wasn't unusual. Now he'd run out of money for a taxi home and he couldn't even use the payphone to ring his Dad to pick him up. Yards away he saw a glint of light reflecting from a coin on the pavement and his eyes lit up. He lurched towards it, and bent down to pick it up.

"Alright love?" said a gruff voice above him.

Darren could tell from the gravity-defying stilettos and the ankles bulging out of them exactly what he was going to be faced with. He stood up to a tottering lady in her mid-forties trying to pout seductively in his direction. The fact that it looked like she was trying to suck an egg through a straw wasn't helped at all by the mini-skirt tucked into her knickers.

"Arrr," said Darren. "I'm alroight ta. Just … errr… dropped me money."

He turned back towards the phone box, he wanted to get away as soon as possible.

"Where are you going?" she continued. "Have you

had a good night? I'm a bit tipsy, **anything** could happen."

Darren felt her hand slide around his waist. He got a lump in his throat, and not in a good way.

"I'm gooing 'om," he replied. "Knackered."

"Home? You can come home with me if you like," she replied in the slow, deliberate way people speak after about five drinks too many. She stared up at Darren, "I'll make it worth your while." Her grin made him shudder.

She stumbled forwards and pulled him to her. He tried to struggle free, but he was completely trapped. He let out a yelp as he felt his squashed kebab oozing down the front of his t-shirt.

"Oi, you!" she called. "Taxi!"

A black cab pulled up next to them. Darren opened the door, let her in and ran away as fast as he could.

Glancing behind as he jogged away, he was relieved when he saw her taxi speed off in the opposite direction. He slowed down to a walk but not before he crashed into a group of girls whom he sent sprawling across the floor.

"Look where you're going!" whined one of the girls as she hauled herself to her feet.

"Oh shut up," said Darren, lashing out and pushing her back to the floor.

He walked off amidst a tirade of insults and stunned spectators to find another phone box. He still had to make his way home.

Stepping inside the phone box on the corner, Darren used the fifty pence he'd found on the floor earlier to ring his Dad. This phone **was** temperamental though and he must have tried to type in his Dad's number five times without being able to get a ring tone. Cursing, he hammered on the side of the receiver with his fist, jolting it into action.

The phone box began to spin, and green smoke filled the air all around him.

* * *

Not many people realise that our marvellous telecoms engineers here in the UK have accidentally invented technology which enables us to travel to parallel dimensions. Even less realise that all it takes to do so is to dial a valid area code, country, galaxy, universe and dimension code, plus the three extra "lucky" 7's needed to activate "Traveller Mode". Darren had managed to type in the number for a lovely little dimension, which personally, I'd love to visit. His 50p ensured him a premium rate connection and a one way journey there.

* * *

The phone box stopped spinning, and settled on the ground. A dazed and confused Darren took a few seconds to compose himself before he stepped out of the phone box into a brand new dimension.

Darren was a giant in a land from a fairy tale. He stood next to a range of hills, none of which seemed to be much bigger than he was. Not too far away he could see a waterfall which gushed a yellow river through a pink rocky façade. He tentatively left the phone box, and walked towards it.

Dry-mouthed from the dodgy kebab earlier, he knelt down next to the river, which could only have been a few feet across, and scooped up the yellow liquid.

"Lemonade?!" he gasped out loud as the bubbles tickled his palms. Sure enough it was, and he drank the sticky, sugary liquid freely from the river. Having quenched his thirst, he lay next to the river for a while to sleep off his night of excess.

Darren woke to a tickling on his face.

"Gerroff Butch," he said, turning over.

"I said, stoppit boy. Cor yer see I'm tired?"

The tickling didn't stop.

"GOO AWAY BUTCH!" he shouted, and was greeted by a loud "mehhr" which quickly spread across the pink field he had fallen asleep in.

Darren sat up groggily. That really didn't sound like his dog. It wasn't, Darren was surrounded by hundreds of miniature black sheep who had crowded around him whilst he was asleep. The more adventurous ones were nibbling at his trousers.

"Gerr away," he chuntered as he swept a few of them away with the back of his hand. A few others moved in to take over nibbling duties, and they were flicked off too.

"Yow don't give up, do yer?" he said, picking one up to have a closer look.

The tiny black, hard and shiny sheep nibbled at his finger. Darren made a sarcastic *baaing* noise and tossed him across the field.

He stood up and stretched, yawning loudly. He could see what seemed like to the ends of the earth from his high perspective. Everything was tiny. He could see forests in the distance, long pink flowing meadows and possibly even a small village in the distance. The only things that seemed normal-sized were some multi-coloured hills on the horizon. He decided to wander along the river towards the village. Darren had little regard for the 'baaing' sheep. Many crunched underfoot, and plenty more were kicked out of the way. They began to scarper fast.

Surprisingly, Darren found that walking along the tiny river was actually quite pleasant. He was actually enjoying being outside, contrary to his usual routine of playing video-games, getting drunk and having a lie-in. It was very rare that he ventured outside at home, he assumed that everywhere was the same as the run down bit of canal he lived by, where all the old factories were desolate and collapsing in on themselves. The only time he ever went outside was to get a hit from one of the drug dealers who frequented the canal bridges and alleyways nearby, or to go up town to get drunk and find girls. Here it was very different. There was a sweet smell in the air, given out by the river, Darren assumed. The path was soft and springy, and there was a peaceful and serene air to the whole place. He also felt quite important, being a giant and everything. Darren may have no idea where he was, but he did quite like it. He was hoping to find some people soon though, he knew he'd get bored otherwise.

Ahead, still far in the distance, was the small village sitting to the side of a colourful hill.

"Excellent," he thought, "I'll be able to get me some food there."

Darren had still got the munchies after having had a skinful last night and losing his kebab thanks to that scary woman.

As he got closer to the village, he began to get a little bit disappointed. It didn't appear to be getting significantly bigger. *I hope it's still far away,* he thought, *I don't want to have to talk to tiny folk.*

He sat down for a little sulk. His feet were hurting and his brain was pounding as his hangover was beginning to set in. Hopeful that a bit of sugar would refresh him, he dragged himself back down to the river for another drink of lemonade. He was amazed when he spotted, across the river, a little bushel of purple trees with candy canes growing on them.

Taking a large step, Darren could just about cross the river in one go. He bent down to the trees, and plucked a candy cane from one of the branches. His hand got covered in a pink pollen, which to his delight he found was icing sugar. Eating the candy cane gave him enough energy to continue his walk to the small village, and he reached it sooner than he had thought.

As Darren had feared, the village was tiny. If there were villagers they would also be miniscule - how was he supposed to talk to them? He could barely see their houses - even they were only a few inches high.

Darren lay down on his pot-belly and propped his head up so that he was staring right into the town. It was still very early in the morning, and there was no-one about. Darren didn't like this, he wanted to see people!

Unable to wait for them to come out, Darren chose a small house next to him, and carefully lifted the roof off. It came off surprisingly easily, and Darren studied it closely. It looked remarkably like a home-made biscuit. Darren took a cautious nibble. *Gingerbread!* He ate the rest of it up quickly, and peered around the rest of the town.

He quickly realised it wasn't just one roof, lots of the houses were made of gingerbread! There was one extremely posh looking building which he was sure was made of custard creams! It looked just like a guesthouse he'd stayed at in Cornwall. He snapped the top off the clock tower in the village square and put it in his mouth. *Dark chocolate! My favourite!* The rest of the clock tower quickly followed.

Glancing around the village he could see many more sweet delights, he felt like he was five years old again. There was one thing in particular that caught his attention though. Tucked up in their beds in the little cottage he had taken the roof off, were five sleeping jelly babies.

He knew it was probably wrong, but he couldn't help it. He reached into the room and took one of the jelly babies out of their bed. It wriggled between his fingertips and began to scream in a shrill voice. The others woke up and joined in.

"Shut yer fizzog!" he shouted, and he placed the jelly baby in his mouth. *Mmmm…Tasty!* he thought.

After eating the whole family, Darren noticed that many of the other doors had opened and jelly babies were spilling out onto the streets.

The whole village is full of jelly babies! he thought with glee.

These jelly babies were all quite angry though, and the air was filled with shrieking. Many of them had pitchforks in their hands which they were waving around with venom.

Darren just grinned, picked another two up and ate them. He grabbed a nearby house, broke it into bits and tossed the pieces casually into his mouth. All of them, the gingerbread walls, candyfloss carpets, jelly sofas, chocolate tables and even lemon sherbet toilets! Quite what was making them fizz he didn't want to think about, but they were tasty all the same.

When he had finished eating, he sat up and casually picked up one or two jelly babies, just for a look. *It's like being God,* thought Darren. He was loving this.

Once he had finished playing around, he got up and went for a further walk. If he was blessed with candy towns, who knows what other delights were in store for him in this world! In the distance he could spy a forest, so he made his way in that direction, eager to see what it was made of.

It didn't take him long, and the trees were equally

delicious. Some were made of chocolate, others icing, some were toffee towers twirled into the sky. Some had delicious fruits, pear drops, cherry jellies or marshmallows. Even more exciting, when Darren ripped a handful out of the ground, he found that the grass was actually candy floss and the earth was chocolate sponge! If he dug deep enough, it was warm and gooey. Darren ate until he could eat no more, and lay on his back holding his stomach. Destruction lay all around him.

Dreams flooded Darren's mind. It was probably the sugar, but there were fairies everywhere, and lands of jellies and cream cakes. He was on a crazy adventure with to infiltrate a castle and rescue a fair maiden by munching through the castle walls and torturing her jelly baby capturers when his sweet dreams were interrupted by a loud "hrummpphh."

He awoke with a start and looked up to see a very annoyed dragon staring down at him.

"You're in biiiiiiiggg trouble," said the dragon.

Darren didn't really say anything, he was in awe. The dragon was huge, and appeared to be in keeping with everything else in this land. She was made of cake!! From her éclair eyebrows to her battenburg neck to the doughnuts and iced buns stuck to her tummy, she was 100% cake. She was far, far bigger than he was, and he wanted to eat her.

Unfortunately, he wasn't sure he was going to get the opportunity.

"I said, you're in big trouble," she repeated.

"I 'eard yow the first time," said Darren, "but what 'ave I dun?"

"What have you done?" said the cake dragon. "What have you done?! You've broked everything! You've smashed up the village, you've pulled up the forest and you've eaten the jelly babies!"

"I were hungry," shrugged Darren.

"You… you … you are.. horrid!!" exclaimed the cake dragon, shaking with anger so much that a vanilla slice on the side of her head wobbled furiously.

Darren looked at it, licking his lips.

The cake dragon had noticed. "What are you doing?" she asked.

"Ermmm nothing.." said Darren.

"Do you…" She wobbled a bit more. "Do you want to **eat** me?" she asked furiously.

"Arrr, a little bit," admitted Darren. "Yow look like a roight tasty bit o' stuff."

That wasn't the first time Darren had used that line, but it was the first time he had used it on a cake dragon. The previous night he'd had a pint of cider tipped on him, not so much for using the line but for the grapple that had accompanied it. It might have had a very different meaning this time, but it got an equally angry reaction and he was pinned to the floor by a jet of squirty cream which roared from the dragon's mouth.

"Daddy!" shouted the cake dragon. "There's a man trying to eat me! DADDY!"

Darren cowered under the cream as a giant shadow enveloped him.

"And what do we have here, Eclair?" asked the cake dragon which dwarfed even the massive Eclair. Darren could barely comprehend how big these creatures were but he knew it had been a bad idea to upset them.

"He's an 'orrible man, Daddy," Eclair the cake dragon continued. "He's been eating the jelly babies, he's broken their houses and he's dug up the forest. And now he wants to eat me!"

"Really Eclair? Well that's quite despicable behaviour."

"Yes it **is** despictable 'haviour," said Eclair, trying to repeat the long words that her Daddy had said.

"So what are we going do with him?"

"Errrmmm…" said Eclair, thinking hard. "I don't know Daddy."

"Do you think we should punish him?"

Eclair didn't need to think about this question. "Yeah! Punish him!"

"Ok." The Daddy cake dragon stood silently, thinking of what else he could suggest. Eventually, "Shall we take him to Mummy?" was the response.

"Yeah!" cried Eclair. "Mummy will know what to do!"

The Daddy cake dragon knelt down, picked Darren up and threw him onto his back. Eclair half scampered, half flew up. She hadn't started flying yet so getting onto his back wasn't the smoothest of operations.

"Hold on tight," said Daddy. "Let's go!

"Wheeee!" shouted Eclair, as they took off into the sky.

It wasn't too long before the novelty of flying wore off Eclair and she started to study Darren.

Darren had already concerned himself with other things. The spine of the cake dragon's back was made of seaside rock, and he was licking it heartily.

"You are eating my Daddy!!" shouted Eclair when she noticed.

Darren gave her a sly wink. That was enough for the baby dragon and she had a little tantrum. She kicked out at Darren and he sailed through the air until he was just a tiny splash in the yellow sea. Eclair went silent, a little bit shocked at what had just happened.

"Eclair?" said the Daddy dragon in a gruff voice. "Did you just throw him into the sea?"

"No, Daddy," she replied. "He fell."

There was a long silence.

"Eclair?"

Eclair knew he would find out. She was a rubbish liar. "Daddy I didn't mean to! He was being mean, he was trying to eat you!"

"We'll talk about this when we land."

"But Daddy, he…"

"Enough!"

Eclair knew what enough meant, and she held onto his back, sobbing and coughing up creamy tears as her Daddy swooped and skimmed the ocean, looking for Darren.

A few minutes later they landed on solid ground, and Eclair rolled off and looked at the floor. She knew she was in trouble.

"Eclair," said the Daddy dragon softly.

"Yes?" she said, gazing upwards into his eyes.

"Do you know what you've done wrong?"

Eclair looked down at her chocolate-taloned feet.

"Yes Daddy. I shouldn't have kicked him, even if he was trying to eat you."

"That's right Eclair, you shouldn't be cruel to any living things even if they are cruel to us. You know this."

"I'm sorry Daddy, I didn't mean for him to fall in the sea."

"Don't apologise to me," he said. "Apologise to him."

Her Daddy threw the sodden Darren onto the candy floss floor, where he bounced a little.

Eclair was delighted to see him, and her guilt evaporated. "I'm sorry!" she cried. "I won't do it again!"

Darren groaned and tried to turn over, but the candy floss grass had started to stick to his wet clothing.

The giant cake dragon looked at him closely with a studious eye. "Have you ever seen anything that looks like that before, Eclair? He is a really rare one, Mummy will be pleased."

Eclair shook her head vigorously. "No, never. I think he's a new one!"

Daddy dragon scooped Darren up and they walked, or more accurately, plodded back towards their home, a huge castle made of pink wafers sitting high on the butterscotch cliffs.

"Mummy!" shouted Eclair excitedly as they reached the drawbridge. "I have a something for you!"

"What, a present?" enquired a huge, multi-coloured cake dragon flying from a high tower to meet them. "For me? Thank you Eclair, that is very kind."

Eclair beamed. "Daddy, show her!"

He placed Darren carefully on the floor, and flicked him towards Mummy. He stumbled to his feet and stared up at her, dumbfounded by her size.

"He's a nasty one," said Eclair "and he must be punished. He was eating the jelly babies!"

"He was what?" said Mummy. "That is very naughty. How do you think we should punish him?"

"I don't know," said Eclair. "We were hoping you had some ideas."

"Hmmm it's tricky, isn't it?" said Mummy. "We could just add him to the collection?"

"Yes!" shouted Eclair, "the collection!"

Mummy picked up Eclair and Daddy picked up Darren, and they flew into the castle. They rushed down a flight of stairs into a cold, damp, spooky cellar, dark except for the flickering candles that they held. Darren looked up at the shelves in front of him. There were rows and rows of bottles, as high and as wide as he could see. In each bottle there was a creature. Cats, dogs, a tiger, a green splodgy figure which he could only relate to an alien. A weird animal that looked to be a cross between a lion and a budgerigar, with a long mane, whiskers and a sharp beak. A tyrannosaurus rex. A hedgehog. A purple stick insect. Everywhere he looked there was a different creature, some specimens he recognised but most he was sure they didn't have back where he came from.

At the end of one shelf there seemed to be a small collection of humans, each one in a separate bottle. Mummy dragon reached up and removed an empty bottle from next to them.

"He can go in here," she said. "What shall we call him? He's obviously one of the spindly straight-backed fleshy babies, but a special kind. A lesser spotted one."

"Yes, a lesser spotted brown haired spindly straight-backed fleshy baby!" cried Eclair.

Mummy dragon nodded, scrawled it on a label which she stuck to the jar. She opened it, popped Darren in and replaced the stopper.

"There we are," she said. "Thank you for my present Eclair. He's a good one."

Eclair laughed. "And he can't get in any more trouble down here, can he?"

Mummy shook her head. The dragons walked across the room and back up the stairs, blowing out the candles as they left.

Matty Millard

If you enjoyed this story about Eclair the Cake Dragon – get more of her story in my novel "In That Other Dimension."

An Incy Wincy Holocaust

It had been a typical birthday.

I went out, as usual, to celebrate with my nearest and dearest. It was nothing fancy, just a gathering in a shabby hall in a desolate part of town. But everyone I cared about was there, my family, my friends and their families. It was a wonderful night. Everyone was having a great time - propped up at the bar laughing and joking, whirling around the dancefloor with their significant other, or just standing around the edge chattering with their friends. The kids scurried around, in and out of the shadows, playing hide and seek in great spirits. It was a thoroughly enjoyable affair - until my worst enemy turned up.

Things soon got ugly.

My friends surrounded me. I was told to "just ignore him." Advised, "don't let him ruin your night." The trouble was that he already had. Even if I'd kept perfectly calm and the red mist hadn't come down, everyone else had noticed his arrival and the atmosphere was quashed. Great tension filled the air as everyone looked to see what I would do.

I didn't really want to do anything. Zarchius, a muscle-bound brute, towered over me. Even though I wasn't small, I was a scrawny wretch in comparison. He had come with five members of his notorious hit squad who were all equally intimidating to the eye. The six of them had tormented the whole village for over a year. Everyone feared them. More than twenty families had lost children to Zarchius, some had been killed, some taken into slavery.

I didn't want to antagonise him, but it was hard not to spit in the face of the scum that had raped my sister.

So I did.

Zarchius looked down at me with an expression of astonishment. He knew we were foolish to take them on. A mass brawl ensued, Zarchius and his five against all those who were at my birthday. Zarchius and his fighters moved elegantly amongst our group, the skilful, highly trained fighters systematically taking down our spirited group of ruffians one by one. It wasn't long before the odds were firmly stacked against us. Zarchius and his crew had been clear favourites even when heavily outnumbered, and our numbers were thinning out quickly.

They attacked together, striking intelligently in waves. They could sense our fragility. We were just a jumbled mess of common thugs and they exploited our weaknesses easily. They weaved in and out, patiently waiting for opportunities. When they spotted one they were inevitably deadly. As I scampered out of the path of one of his cronies, I glimpsed Zarchius across the room. I'd seen him a few times, and he always saw me. He constantly watched me in his peripheral vision, watching for the perfect chance to make me pay for my show of insolence.

It wasn't long before he spotted a path through the melee, and he dashed through it. Zarchius flung my friends and family out of his way as if they weren't there, and charged straight for me. I dodged but stumbled. Wriggling back to my feet I breathed heavily as Zarchius turned around to face me again.

Zarchius raised an arm to strike. I found myself paralysed with fear, watching him instead of thinking what I should do next. He knew that I was his for the taking, and struck with speed and venom. I was finished - had my brother not tackled me out of the way. We rolled together to the other side of the room, untangled ourselves and readied for the next attack.

Zarchius scowled at me and charged, the anger flared across his face. This time I reacted, scrambling to my feet just in time and lunging awkwardly to the side. Somehow I struck out with my foot, and connected well. Really well. Zarchius stumbled in surprise and twisted his leg horribly, snapping it in two. But still he still fought on, dragging his useless leg around the room, still trying to get at me. He fought bitterly but my friends saw his weakness and piled in. Zarchius, for so long the tormenter of our society, was ripped to pieces.

Seeing their leader fallen, his hit squad scuttled away, cowardly and pathetic without him.

The room erupted. Our village's most feared and hated tormenter was dead! Despite the huge losses which had been suffered, vigorous celebrations ensued, the likes of which I've never seen before.

The congratulations and thanks just kept coming. A female I barely knew jumped on top of me. I had to physically restrain her just to maintain some public decency. It wasn't the only offer I had that night, and the whole day quickly became a blur of memories and emotions.

In hindsight, it was almost exactly the birthday I had expected. A fight to the death and a suitably impressed girl for the winner was standard fare in our neighbourhood. I just hadn't expected, or wanted, to fight Zarchius.

I saw my brother pushing his way through the crowds. I greeted him, beaming widely. We had wanted Zarchius dead for months.

"You shouldn't have done that," admonished Simeon. "You're a complete and utter idiot…"

"But I won!" I contested. "I killed Zarchius! He's out of our lives forever."

"That's not the point," he spat. "There was too much at stake tonight. Just think what would have happened if you had lost…"

I knew he was right, I'd have told him exactly the same thing had our roles been reversed.

"I'm sorry," I mumbled, looking down at the floor.

"Cortis, I'm glad he's dead," my brother continued with more than a glint of hatred in his eyes. "You have done our family a great service. But we can't lose sight of what we need to do tomorrow. You are the key to our plans."

I nodded, still looking at the floor. My rashness had been selfish, I knew. My brothers and I had big plans. Massive plans. Plans which would cement the future of our family and ensure our survival in this stark and unforgiving world. But my petulance had nearly ruined everything. If I had died, the plans were over.

"I know," I sighed. "I'll be more careful in future I promise."

"I know you will," Simeon continued kindly. "And

thank you. We will never forget what you did tonight."

I looked at him and we shared a moment of solemn victory. Sombrely, we turned and left the raucous party to go back home. My thoughts returned to our plan. "I must focus," I told myself. Tomorrow would change the lives of each and every member of my family.

* * *

Let me tell you about our plan. First of all though, you need a little perspective.

For hundreds of years the entire Earth has been ruled by the Neo-Communist Kring Dynasty, a cruel and controlling regime which has transformed humanity.

Over this time, the Dynasty cultured two million Kring Commanders through a painstakingly patient and brutal brainwashing and terror programme.

The Kring Commanders were the most loyal and obedient men that had ever existed. Many sacrificed their lives for the General. They were the perfect servants, unquestioning and devoted in everything they did. They knew it was all for the common good.

On the 20th of August, 2731 AD, General Kring launched the nukes. This was the Ultimate Solution, the step that would bring Perfect Equality to the Earth. With a promise of a place in the final race of equals, the Kring Commanders had seen to it that every building in the towns they governed was vulnerable to the radiation. There were little pockets of resistance, small groups who believed something untoward was coming. Their bunkers were demolished and their voices quashed.

Whilst missiles exploded all over the Earth, Kring's chosen sat safely in the fallout shelter his servants had built. Every human, every animal, every bird and every insect was killed. What remained of the fast receding oceans became still and empty. Life as it had been on Earth for thousands of years, was no more.

And with that one act of destruction, Kring achieved the ultimate goal of his Neo-Communist dynasty.

Every member of the human race was now equal.

* * *

In my opinion, humanity has become a pitiful race. I have heard stories from the past when they used to walk places, feed themselves and communicate verbally. Nowadays every human is motionless. They are controlled by an internal electronic device, the LifeUnit, which reacts to sensory responses from their brain. Through this LifeUnit they can perform any of the actions they used to. Instead of talking, the technology trades messages without the need for their lips to move. They can walk and move their limbs by simply thinking about it, but not by using any muscles. Their robotic limbs do everything they need.

I have to admit, General Kring is a clever man as were his predecessors. To convert a race born to eat and breed into one which needs no more sustenance than that their robotic limbs provide is remarkable. Since the nuclear holocaust the human race has thrived, and General Kring has been mechanically cloned time and time again. The population has reached almost one million already. One million identical clones of General Kring, none of whom have any physical capability at all. One million people with the same thoughts, the same personality and the same will. There is no person who is stronger than another, mentally, physically or financially. There are no individuals, aside from the original General Kring of course, who can choose to make more clones. That's as Perfect Equality as you will ever see.

Despite his promises to his Commanders, General Kring was the only living creature he had chosen to survive the holocaust. He was the only one meant to survive, and as far as he knows, he is the only one to survive.

He doesn't know about me.

* * *

Twenty years ago, my Great-Great-Great-Great Grandmother was roaming the empty streets when it began to rain. It had been a fairly normal day thus far, but the day became eventful when she heard a robotic humanoid striding through the town. This was a rare sight nowadays as humans no longer had any need to go outside. Everything they needed in life was provided through their mechanical core.

This particular human was General Kring. Little did my Great-Great-Great-Great Grandmother know that he had just been out to initialise the nuclear sequence that would deliver his Perfect Equality. Luckily for her, and me, the rain drove her indoors and she snuck into the leaden room from which General Kring observed the destruction of all life on the planet.

The destruction of all life on Earth, except for himself and my heavily pregnant Great-Great-Great-Great Grandmother who was hiding in a shadowy corner of the room.

Two days later she gave birth to two-thousand four-hundred and fifty-three children, who quickly grew up and bred themselves. Contrary to the humans, they were not linked up to any electronic LifeUnit which automatically fed and cloned them. A horrible cycle of cannibalism and incest was necessary for the survival of my species. Two despicable practices which had been wiped out of our civilised society hundreds of years ago were resurrected.

I **hate** General Kring for forcing my people to resort to such desperate actions.

General Kring had an almost flawless plan to create his perfect world where no-one has any advantage over another. His aim for a world without conflict, without superiority and without jealousy. He used technology to achieve what nobody had thought was possible, but he forgot about two important factors.

Firstly, basic human error. If you're aiming to wipe all life forms from the face of the Earth, it is important to check that my Great-Great-Great-Great Grandmother isn't hiding in the corner.

And secondly, the power of evolution.

General Kring had forgotten about the power that nature has to overcome all odds. No matter what technology is used, life will always find a way to win. His holocaust forced my ancestors to degrade themselves for survival, but the need for my family to eat each other brought on an inevitable change. I am the first spider in the whole of this new world to have teeth.

Big, sharp, yellow fangs.

I am a member of a previously harmless species, who can now deliver the most venomous bite the Earth has ever seen.

Prior to the holocaust, us spiders were scared of humans. Millions of innocent spiders were drowned every year, and worst of all humans used to taunt us with songs.

"The Incy Wincy Spider, climbed up the water spout..."

I absolutely **hate** that song. We all know that that the

spider can't really climb up the spout again when he's dead, we're not stupid. It wasn't enough that humans killed us for no reason, they had to celebrate it too.

But now, General Kring, things have changed. We're not scared any more.

You killed my ancestors and you tried to destroy the world. You forced my family into unspeakable acts of self-depreciation just to survive. You have made us live with an undeterminable guilt and feeling of self-loathing.

General Kring, I absolutely detest the human race.

Three weeks after the holocaust, when you opened the air vents to allow more of your breathable air in, you opened up the world to us spiders. Big mistake.

Because now, General Kring, I am coming to get you. Every single sick and twisted god-damn copy of you.

I will not rest until I have spilled the blood of every last human on Earth and injected it with my deadly venom. I will sit and watch every one of you squirm in vicious pain, as the poison infiltrates your pathetically weak bodies. I will enjoy as your bodies twist, writhe and eventually fall limp, even the infallible LifeUnit unable to save you. Then I will introduce my family to their new and plentiful source of nutrition – lovely, warm, rich and wholesome human blood.

I can only imagine it will taste sweet, like revenge.

Matty Millard

FREEDOM

The man howled in derision as the whip split open his scarred and withered back. Looking upwards into the cold and heartless eyes of his Master, he knew he was going to get no sympathy. It was the same every day, work until you drop or are beaten into unconsciousness.

For thirteen years the man had been enslaved in the mines. He had once had a family, friends, a purpose. He had once had a name.

"Jack."

For the first ten years of imprisonment he could hear his wife whispering it to him across the coffee table on their first, life-changing date. Even that memory had left him now.

It had been eight years since Jack had seen sunlight. He had only seen it then because one of the coal wagons had toppled and someone had to go outside to reload it. That had been his best day in slavery.

Jack hadn't washed since the day he was abducted, driving his apple cart to his local village. The slaves lived in the mines in their own filth. Occasionally they were given water, but they weren't going to wash. Their never-ending thirst was more important than their cleanliness. Jack had puss oozing out of a gash on his shoulder-blade, and a family of maggots living in his tangled beard. At least there was still some life in him somewhere, he supposed.

They were all the same, the men down there. Some were newer, teary-eyed and desperate for their lives back. They had hope. Others, like Jack, had been there for years and were numb to the core. Even if they got out there would be no life, not after this. All they wanted was for their nightmares to end.

Every day was the same ritual; a never ending cycle. Woken up early in the morning, the men were kicked out of their beds if they were too sluggish. They were thrown water and stale bread for breakfast, if they were lucky. Jack didn't always get any, sometimes the other men had fought over it like savage animals before he even had the chance. The uniformed soldiers, smug, callous and uncaring, came to drag the slaves along the winding passages, deeper underground into the mine shaft. There, every man was worked until they could work no more.

Jack was at that point now. Straining and shaking from fourteen hours of hard labour without a single break, even for water, he thrust his pick weakly towards the wall. Falling just short he collapsed under the weight and landed face down in the dust. There was no crack of the whip this time. Through the slits of his barely open eyes, he saw his Master baring his teeth at him in disgust. He couldn't do any more, he had nothing left. His Master picked him up by his hair and threw him back to the floor. Jack's world went dark.

Hours later, Jack awoke in agony. Every bone in his body ached but he didn't dare to cry out in pain. The sacking that kept him from sleeping straight on the cold stone floor gave him no comfort. Packed tightly around him lay the other slaves. Many were unconscious - the body's only way to recuperate ready for the toils of the following day.

Except today was different.

Today, Jack was going to get out. This place; dark, claustrophobic and cruel, would not control him any more. Today was the day this would change. He was going to get out.

A stubborn determination taking over him, Jack hauled his body upright, pain screaming through his shoulder. Around him, the broken stirred wearily. One soul-less skeleton next to him was staring at him in disbelief. The eyes in his shrivelled up sockets flashed petrified warnings. If Jack got caught moving around he would be beaten senseless for days.

Jack ignored the silent protests of the men he stumbled across. They were fools, all of them. Weak, pathetic fools for allowing those bullies to reduce them to this. *"Get some self respect for pity's sake"* he thought, forgetting in his single-minded determination that he was one of them.

He made his way across the room to the huge wooden door which separated them from the outside world. It was inches thick, Jack knew that. There were heavy chains on the other side, keeping them locked in. There was no way of breaking it down, though many had tried.

Surveying the room one last time, Jack's eyes began to fill with tears. All around the room were sacks full of coal, freshly mined by the slaves that day. Crammed in between the sacks were hundreds of men, all broken and helpless. Every single one of them had once had hopes, ambitions and dreams. They must have had friends too, and loved ones. Now look at them. They were nothing, they were lifeless, they were empty carcasses. The lights in their eyes had faded. They had no minds of their own, no thoughts, nothing.

Jack was about to take another decision from them and he felt guilty for it, but this decision was for the better. Jack knew he couldn't tell anyone, he had to do this alone. If people knew, someone would be scared and would stop him. That couldn't happen. This was Jack's only chance to be free from his fear, free from his self-loathing and free from his horrendous existence.

Jack lit the match his Master had dropped earlier when he was busy beating him. Jack hadn't been able to believe his luck, even the soldiers weren't allowed matches in the mines. His hand shaking uncontrollably, Jack held it as still as he could under the corner of one of the sacks. Praying for God's mercy he was rewarded as the fire took hold.

Joyous and liberated, Jack sank to his knees. "You will not control me any more!" he cried in victory. Grasping the only possession he had left, he knelt and wept. Even though the photo was weathered and covered in dirt and charcoal, he could still see the outline of his beautiful wife and daughter smiling back at him.

While the rest of the prisoners awoke and ran amok in confused terror, Jack stared happily at the only memory he wanted to take away with him from this life. Contented as the cleansing flames flickered around the chamber, he gazed in wonder at their powerful beauty. Before his very eyes he could see his turmoil and worries turning to ashes, and floating gently away.

As the heat grew, the coals crackled and the flames hissed at Jack's feet, he thought he heard his wife whisper his name one last time. "Jack..."

Jack lay back and slept in peace. He finally had what he had desired for so long.

Jack had his freedom back.

IF YOU ENJOYED THIS…

Please check out my novel, In That Other Dimension. It's a crazy romp through parallel dimensions starring the cake dragon Eclair, who you met earlier. It's available on Amazon, paperback or ebook.

Come say hi! All my social / website links are below:

https://linktr.ee/matty_millard

ABOUT THE AUTHOR

It's been 8 years since my first publication, and life has changed a bit. I'm no longer writing in the kitchen because my brother has taken over my office, I'm writing in short bursts morning and night, hoping I get something done before the children wake up.

This is my first short story collection. I find short stories hard, but rewarding. You can do more in a short story because you don't need to keep characters likeable, or even alive, for a whole 200 pages.

As a child brought up on Enid Blyton and Roald Dahl, followed by Douglas Adams and Terry Pratchett, I have a special sense of humour. I've got more into sci-fi in recent years and enjoy Philip K Dick and Kurt Vonnegut. Hopefully some of these influences come through in my writing.

So, are you going to get another novel from me? Hopefully – one day soon. I've written two more but editing is so boring! I know that's not a great excuse but there are more fun things to do now that I have two little boys. But seriously, I will finish them – editing of Aliens.exe is already well under way.

Anyway – it's nice to be published again. If you enjoyed this book then please leave me a review. You probably don't realise how pleasing it is to hear that someone likes your writing – not to mention how vital reviews are in making your books visible on Amazon.

Thanks for your support,
Matty

ALIENS.EXE – A SNEAK PEEK!

Chapter 1 - The Beginning

In the deepest, darkest, narrowest crevasse of the third-largest crater on the Moon of Everlasting Lightning was a little hamlet called Schmingleton. In Schmingleton lived seventeen people, none of whom had ever achieved anything of any note. Twelve of them were males born to the same mother. They lived in a three bedroomed semi and had no father. Some would say that their Mom, Teresa, was unlucky to have had so many immaculate conceptions. Others would say she was enlightened. Most would say she was completely irrelevant to this story, so quite frankly, who cares?

Living next door to this full to bursting house was a wiry young man called Jake. Jake hated the Teresons, as they were known in Schmingleton. They were noisy, obnoxious, riotous and vulgar. They acted like they owned the place and they made his life a misery, stealing his deliveries and banging on his front door. The Tereson's had instilled such fear into Jake that he hadn't left his house in thirteen weeks. An already skinny and underweight man was becoming a weak and frail skeleton. His emergency supply of crisps had run out three days ago and things were getting desperate. Even his routine licking of each packet was now proving fruitless, he survived solely on salted fumes.

Jake, however, was past caring. His passion for life was long gone, the Teresons had seen to that. His day to day routine of signing into internet chat-rooms, moaning about his terrible life and storming out in an attention-seeking barrage of foul-mouthed abbreviations was over. He barely had the willpower to turn his monitor off every night before bed any more.

Jake was going to end it all. There was just no point going on. He didn't eat, he didn't sleep, he didn't communicate and he didn't care. He was 1000% sure this was the end of everything, and virtually everyone he virtually knew, knew it as well.

Jake's final day had been fast approaching for a long while, and today was that day.

Chapter 2 - The End

Although a good for nothing, manically depressed layabout, Jake did have one good quality. He never broke a promise. He had but one true friend in the world. Green_Turtle_Boy_369 had been his friend for years, beginning in the computerised world of Lapine Death Corps where they had both made it to 15,000 gamer points on the same day. Ever since this momentous occasion, Jake and Green_Turtle_Boy_369 had been firm friends and had played together regularly, sometimes fiercely competitive but sometimes co-operating to blast the hell out of fearless zombie rabbits in a flamboyantly efficient fashion that even the finest poetry couldn't do justice to describe. Jake knew that the one thing in life he would miss was Green_Turtle_Boy_369's smiley face emoticon. He almost smiled himself at the thought, but his face was so contorted from licking crisp packets that it was more like a wonky wink. *Green_Turtle_Boy_369 used to do that sometimes too*, he thought, reflecting on his good friend's cheeky and jovial nature.

Jake's one good quality then, would today be tested by a promise he made to Green_Turtle_Boy_369. It had been at least three weeks since Green_Turtle_Boy_369 had signed into their most frequented chat-room disguised as "Pleasure_Girl_4_U", an open minded lesbian who had coaxed the hate, self-loathing and suicidal truth out of Jake. After hearing the extent of Jake's depression, Green_Turtle_Boy_369 had admitted his misdemeanour, and had made Jake promise that if he did ever end his life, that he would do so by running a small program that he had written. Before Jake's computer exploded, killing him swiftly, the program would send a virus out to all of the computers in the outer galaxies, thus rendering them completely useless. This would allow Green_Turtle_Boy_369 to lead a revolution to overpower the fascist dictatorship of the Grand Zombie-Master, who had decreed that only zombie rabbits were allowed in their beloved Lapine world. Green_Turtle_Boy_369 was bored of zombie rabbits, from time to time he just wanted to shoot some god-damn aliens. When the program had finished, Green_Turtle_Boy_369 would receive a pop-up message box to tell him that it had worked.

Jake was a loyal guy, and had remembered his promise. He was ready. At least there was one thing he could do with his life to leave a lasting impression behind.

"This one's for you, Green_Turtle_Boy_369," said Jake. He closed his eyes and double-clicked.

Chapter 3 - Another Ending

"Oh shit," said Jake, opening his disappointed eyes at the distinct lack of explosion. "I missed."

Jake's pathetically weak and shaking index finger had sidled off course and he had accidentally opened up his emails instead of ending his life. Jake hated checking his emails. Not only because real people that he'd actually met in real life used them, like his Mom, but because it took a really long time for the program to open. Cursing like a trooper whilst frantically pressing CTRL, ALT + DELETE on his keyboard, Jake tried to stop any new emails showing up.

Too late.

There was just the one, sent four months earlier on the 23rd September entitled "Happy 30th Birthday Sweetie!!" It was from his Mom.

"Why won't she leave me alone!!" screamed Jake, pounding his fist against the desk in anger. Jake took his self-prescribed exclusion from society extremely seriously, and hated anyone who interfered with this. Two years ago, he'd given his Mom strict instructions that if she was ever to speak to him it must be under the user-name "Empress_Of_Dominion" in Lapine Death Corps. She just didn't respect him at all.

Anyway, today wasn't about her or any of the others.

Today was Jake's triumphant ending, and he wasn't going to let anybody spoil it for him.

Jake minimised his emails. With remarkable poise he collected himself and allowed his cursor to hover over Green_Turtle_Boy_369's program, Aliens.exe.

Taking deep breaths, Jake calmly double-clicked his destiny. There was a puff of smoke, and the world went black.

***

I hope you enjoyed this preview into "Aliens.exe". It will be launched on October 27th 2023 – you can buy it using the QR code below. I promise that you'll quickly find out what happened to Jake. It's a rollercoaster ride to say the least!

Matty Millard